Especially for:

TO SHAPE A LIFE

By Melissa Forney

Illustrated by Judy Richardson

Barker Creek Publishing, Inc.
Poulsbo, Washington

Library of Congress Cataloging-in-Publication Data

Forney, Melissa 1952-
    To shape a life: a tribute to teachers / by Melissa Forney;
    illustrated by Judy Richardson.
        p.   cm.
ISBN: 1-928961-03-7
1. Teacher-student relationships—Fiction. 2. Nursing home patients
—Fiction. 3. Aged women—Fiction. 4. Teachers—Fiction.
I. Richardson, Judy. II. Title

PS3556.O7347T6 2000
813'.6—dc21   00-034293

BARKER CREEK
Printed in Hong Kong
First Edition
1 2 3 4 5 6 7 8 9 10
Book design by Judy Richardson
barkercreek.com

This book is dedicated to those who seldom see the long-range fruits of their labor and wonder if, indeed, they made a difference.

In a land of incredible progress, a land where time does not stand still, a dwelling was built for those who had served their usefulness and must now take their rest.

It was called a nursing home, and the aged residents, from all walks of life, occupied themselves with a variety of relaxing activities.

But, try as they might, they remained a lonely lot, faced with a sense of physical limitation, and their own mortality.

In the afternoon, the elderly residents sat in the shade of the front porch, reminiscing about their lives, ruminating among old memories.

"I was an important executive," began an octogenarian. "Among the leaders of our corporation, there was none more powerful than I. No decision was made without my consultation, and I made and destroyed the careers of others. Men trembled before me."

"What were you called?" asked a listener.

"Power," he answered. "What else?"

"Excuse me, sir," said a kind young nurse. "I hate to interrupt, but it's time for your bath." Leaning over, she lifted his frail frame, as light as a child's, and placed him in his wheelchair. "Let's get you cleaned up so you'll look fresh."

"Why?" replied the fretful voice. "I've been here for years and never had a visitor. What difference does it make? Besides," he complained, "I'm too weak today."

In the ensuing silence, another voice filled the void.

"Ah . . . Sweet Youth. I could turn heads in my time. When I performed, they came great distances to see me, throwing roses at my feet at each curtain call. Why, I couldn't get into the dressing room afterwards for the crush of admirers. Men fell to their knees before me."

Momentarily unaware of the other residents, she once again heard the roar of the crowd and the admiring applause of the audience. She savored the image in dreamy enjoyment.

"What were you called?" a man asked, pulling her back to the present.

"Isn't it obvious?" she flirted, once again attempting to play the coquette. "I was called Beauty." The reverie faded as she stared at the backs of her hands, as if seeing them for the first time. "But now I am wrinkled, old and lonely. Where are the fans ? Where are those who once rushed to claim even a moment of my time?"

"I know just what you mean," echoed another. "A rich man has many friends as long as his pockets jingle. The money I made filled the greatest banks of commerce. My investments turned into Midas' gold. I hoarded, stockpiled, bought and sold. Men grovelled before me. No object or product was beyond my buying capabilities." He grew quiet, reflecting.

"What were you called?" asked a curious bystander.

"Wealth," he announced. "Somehow, that's no comfort to me now. I learned the hard way that the most important things in life can't be bought with money."

As his words echoed through the afternoon breeze, a car pulled up, parking beneath the shade of the elms. A tall, striking young woman emerged with a beautifully wrapped package. Making her way to an elderly woman sitting apart from the others, she kissed her softly on the forehead and placed the lovely gift in her lap.

"You probably don't remember me," she said, "but I want to thank you. I went to college and finished law school because of your encouragement. You told me I could do it, and you were right."

The old woman squinted closely as recognition gradually dawned. "Of course! I still recall your graduation speech. Hard work pays off, doesn't it? You'll do more still. Remember, any job worth doing is worth doing well."

As the visitor descended the steps of the porch, she was passed by a family carrying a basket of flowers. "Hello, Mrs. Porter," the husband said to the aged woman. "I wanted to bring my family by to see you."

"Dad, is this the woman who told you all those stories about *Treasure Island* and *A Tale of Two Cities*?"

"It sure is," replied his father. "Thank you, Mrs. Porter, for opening up the world of reading to me. I've been able to pass that love along to my own children."

She pulled her sweater a little closer around her shoulders. "You always did love the classics, Benny," she replied, her voice redolent with memories. "I still remember your book report on the *The Count of Monte Cristo*. Keep reading," she reminded. "We're never lonely with a good book in hand."

"I'll keep that in mind," said the father. "We'll visit more next time. I think someone important is here to see you."

Sure enough, a long limousine had pulled up in front of the building, flanked by dark-suited men talking into walkie-talkies.

From the back seat emerged a distinguished man with handsome good looks and an air of authority. He ascended the steps to face the older woman and tenderly took her by the hand.

"So good to see you again," she crooned proudly.

"I'm addressing the nation tomorrow," he confided.

"You'll do fine. Just remember, get to the point, speak with clarity, and don't end a sentence with a preposition."

He listened intently. "This job is difficult. More than I bargained for."

She considered his words. "You can do it. I've always believed in you."

"You were the only one sometimes."

"Stand tall," she instructed. "Your office demands great integrity and honor."

One of his colleagues announced, "Excuse me, Sir. We must keep on schedule."

The distinguished guest looked into the eyes of his mentor. "I owe you such a debt of gratitude."

"Then make me proud," she challenged. "We're all counting on you."

As the entourage sped away, the elderly woman rocked contentedly. The other residents on the porch talked in urgent and hushed tones, occasionally glancing her way.

"Say!" cried one, finally. "What did you do with your life?"

"What did I do with my life?" she repeated reflectively, pausing to consider the question before answering.

"Can you imagine what it's like to help shape a life? I, too, knew a life of power, beauty, and wealth. I invested in the lives of children, and it has paid off in handsome dividends which will compound for generations to come.

"More children than I could ever count sat in my lap over the years, patting my cheeks and stroking my hair. The gathering wrinkles never seemed to matter. To them, I was as beautiful as a budding rose or raindrops on fresh, dewy grass.

"I experienced the power of training young minds to read the pages of a book and tender hands to write their first halting letters.

"In my job, I had to be at work early, stay late and take work home. I had to produce, manufacture, invent, salvage, transport, motivate, assess, create, congratulate, and challenge. My job combined the skills of psychologist, chauffeur, chef, artist, doctor, scientist, mathematician, coach, musician, and . . . professional wrestler."

An impressed hush fell over the residents.

"What were you called?" came the inevitable question.

$\mathbb{P}$ulling herself up to her full height, she replied
with satisfaction, "I was called . . . Teacher."

Also by Melissa Forney

A Medal for Murphy

No Regard Beauregard and the Golden Rule

Dynamite Writing Ideas!

The Writing Menu

Oonawassee Summer

Blue Tattoo